For Dada

Bear Cub Books
One Park Street
Rochester, Vermont 05767
www.InnerTraditions.com

Bear Cub Books is a division of Inner Traditions International

Text copyright © 2004 by Vatsala Sperling
Artwork copyright © 2004 by Harish Johari and Pieter Weltevrede

LIBRARY OF CONGRESS CATALOGING-IN-PUBLICATION DATA

Johari, Harish, 1934–1999
How Parvati won the heart of Shiva / Harish Johari and Vatsala Sperling ; illustrated
by Pieter Weltevrede.
p. cm.
ISBN 1-59143-042-9
1. Parvati (Hindu diety)—Juvenile literature. 2. Shiva (Hindu diety)—Juvenile literature.
I. Sperling, Vatsala, 1961–   II. Weltevrede, Pieter. III. Title.
BL 1225.P3J64 2004
294.5'13—dc
2004010328

Printed and bound in China

10 9 8 7 6 5 4 3 2 1

Text design and layout by Mary Anne Hurhula
Text layout by Virginia Scott Bowman
This book was typeset in Berkeley with Abbess as the display typeface

Cast of Characters

Mena ('May-na)
Wife of Himalaya,
mother of Parvati

Adishakti ('A-dee-'shak-tee)
The great mother
goddess, Shiva's wife
in heaven

Himalaya (Hi-ma-lay-'a)
King of the Mountains,
husband of Mena,
father of Parvati

Parvati ('Par-va-tee)
An earthly form of
Adishakti, Shiva's
betrothed on Earth

Vishnu ('Vish-noo)
God of Preservation

Indra ('In-dra)
King of the lesser
gods, ruler of rain
and storms

**Shiva (Shee-'va) God
of Destruction and
Lord of All Gods,
Adishakti's husband
in heaven, Parvati's
betrothed on Earth

Kama ('Ka-ma)
The god of earthly
love and desire

Sage Narada ('Nah-rah-da)
A holy spirit and
wise counselor

Rati (Ra-'tee)
Wife of Kama

Brahma (Brahm-'ha)
God of Creation

About Shiva and Parvati

The Hindu people believe that long, long ago in the ancient land of India, gods and goddesses came from Heaven to Earth to take the form of human beings whenever they wanted to. Even though they looked like humans and lived like humans, they had many amazing powers that were not at all human. They could turn into animals or trees or rocks—and then back to human form—whenever they needed to. The gods and goddesses also appeared in the dreams of people who worshipped them and gave these people special favors called boons. The people who received boons could do magical things too.

Stories from these ancient times are told and retold in India to this day. The story you are about to read is about an eternally married couple, the great mother goddess Adishakti and her heavenly husband Shiva (Lord of All Gods). Besides being married in Heaven, whenever Shiva and Adishakti choose to take human form on Earth, they find each other and get married again. In this story Adishakti comes to Earth as the princess Parvati, while Shiva visits Earth as a wandering holy man, or yogi. Parvati knows that Shiva is the only man for her but he's so busy meditating she can't even get him to look at her, let alone marry her.

The story actually begins with Mena, a girl who was renowned for her worship of Shiva and who later became the earthly mother of Parvati.

Mena was a young princess who was devoted to Lord Shiva with all her heart. Pleased with Mena's true devotion, Shiva had granted her a special boon—the ability to be magically transported to any place she wanted to go. Mena was happy to worship Shiva from afar but her secret desire was to see him face to face someday. So when she heard that Lord Vishnu had invited all the gods and sages to his island in Heaven for a visit, she was very excited. Shiva was a dear friend of Vishnu's. Surely he would be there! All she had to do was use her special boon, and go to the heavenly island herself. Her heart thumped with joy and anticipation, and off she flew.

Mena appeared first before Vishnu, whose kindness and hospitality were well known. He looked at her face, shining with love for Shiva. With a kind smile, he said, "Would you like to stay and meet my friends? Shiva will be here soon."

Mena's devotion to Shiva was so great that just the *thought* of actually seeing him put her under his spell, and she sank to the ground in a trance. As the gods and sages began to arrive for the gathering, she did not even notice their arrival. If the sages had known that Mena was under Shiva's spell, they would have understood why she didn't rise to greet them. But not knowing, they shook their old gray heads and grumbled disapprovingly. "These young folk! What disrespect!" And before Vishnu had a chance to explain, one of those wise old sages muttered under his breath, "Since you can't even get up when we come in, rude girl, one day you will end up marrying a mountain!"

When she had regained her senses, poor Mena apologized profusely and begged to be forgiven, but the curse could not be undone. She returned to Earth and roamed the land, lamenting her fate. "How can I possibly marry a mountain?" she cried. Finally, years later, she reached Himalaya, King of the Mountains. Himalaya, too, had been granted a boon from the gods that allowed him to change his form when he needed to. Most of the time he appeared as a jagged mountain range that ran from east to west, and that was how Mena found him. His mountains were the loftiest in the world, the highest peaks always capped with snow. Lower down, the foothills were covered with lush trees, and in springtime the melting snow filled rivers and ponds with fresh, cool water. Many sages lived and meditated in Himalaya's numerous caves.

Lord Shiva himself often came to Earth, taking the form of a wandering yogi. He wore nothing but animal skins, with snakes around his neck and a crescent moon in his long, unruly hair. Shiva favored the most remote places he could find, and especially loved the quiet, intense cold on Mt. Kailash, the tallest of all the snow-covered peaks of Himalaya's mountain range. With Shiva as his honored guest, Himalaya was happy and content.

But when Himalaya felt the lovely Mena wandering across his spine and heard her laments, the desire for a wife grew in his heart and he hastened to appear before her in human form. Himalaya was very handsome indeed, and he was a wise soul as well. He and Mena exchanged stories, both mentioning their devotion to Shiva, and Mena began to feel that marrying a mountain might not be such a bad idea after all.

Soon Mena and Himalaya were wed. Because they both wanted children, they said a special prayer to the great mother goddess Adishakti, inviting her into their lives. Adishakti was so pleased with their prayers that she resolved to be born on Earth as their daughter. In Heaven Adishakti was Shiva's wife. When she came of age on Earth she would find Shiva and marry him again, as always. Of course, the new parents had no idea that their future daughter would grow up to be Shiva's betrothed.

When Mena gave birth to a baby girl, she and Himalaya were overjoyed, and named their child Parvati. Parvati grew to be a beautiful and independent little girl, the apple of her devoted parents' eyes.

When she was a little older, Himalaya presented Parvati with a magical flying carriage. "This will take you anywhere you'd like to go and bring you home safely," he told her. The carriage was made of gold and looked like a little floating palace. Its pillars were decorated with sweet blossoming flowers and its dome was covered with exquisite pearls. Its floor was made of transparent gemstones, and the whole fantastic contraption was powered by the sun. When Parvati traveled in her magic carriage, all eyes turned toward the sky and the mountain people waved to their beloved princess flying by.

While Parvati was still quite young, Sage Narada visited Himalaya. Narada could travel at the speed of light, reaching great distances in the blink of an eye. Very smartly, he kept the entire cosmos under his intense observation. His visits were famous because he always brought news from far-off places. He also liked to point out things that people hadn't realized before, pushing people to take action. Himalaya welcomed Narada with joy and humility—and maybe a little apprehension. He brought Parvati to meet the sage and said, "O Narada, would you please read my daughter's horoscope?"

Narada carefully watched the child and studied her horoscope. Then he cleared his throat. "Himalaya," he began, "your daughter has all the auspicious signs on her body and her horoscope is powerful. She will only bring you joy. But . . . ," he cleared his throat again, "I do see one difficulty. Her husband will be a naked yogi. He will be free from all desires and needs. He will not have any parents. His appearance and manners will be offensive and frightening."

Himalaya broke in, anxious and afraid. "What can I do to help my daughter? Is there a way out?" he asked.

Narada quickly finished explaining. "Do not worry. Parvati's bridegroom will be none other than Lord Shiva. You must make certain that she doesn't marry anyone else."

Himalaya was confused. "But Shiva sits in the wilderness in deepest meditation. He has no interest in women or marriage. How will my daughter succeed in getting his attention, let alone in winning his heart?"

"I see that you are unaware of your daughter's true identity—she is none other than Goddess Adishakti herself, Shiva's eternal wife," answered Narada. Himalaya adored his daughter all the more, now that he knew who she really was. But he kept Narada's revelation to himself.

One day, years later, Mena said to Himalaya, "It is time to find a husband for our daughter." She gazed fondly at Parvati, who had grown into a truly lovely young woman.

Himalaya turned to her gravely. "Mena, my dearest, you must teach her how to pray to Shiva. For it is he who will be her bridegroom."

Mena's eyes filled with hot tears. She knew that being devoted to Shiva was no easy task. Nobody loved Shiva more than she did, and in all these years she had never even gotten to *see* him. How could she put her daughter through such disappointment? But Himalaya told her Narada's predictions, and so she agreed to talk to their daughter. She took Parvati aside to explain gently. "You must do all you can to make Shiva happy with you. He is going to be your husband."

Meanwhile, Shiva had decided to settle on one of Himalaya's lovely mountain peaks to begin a new round of meditation. As soon as he realized that Shiva was nearby, King Himalaya brought Parvati to him. Parvati placed a gift of flowers and fruits before Shiva and stood silently. Himalaya spoke with reverence. "O Lord Shiva, I am honored by your visit. I have asked that no man, beast, or bird should trespass and disturb you. Please, let my daughter, Parvati, serve you and take care of all your needs while you are here."

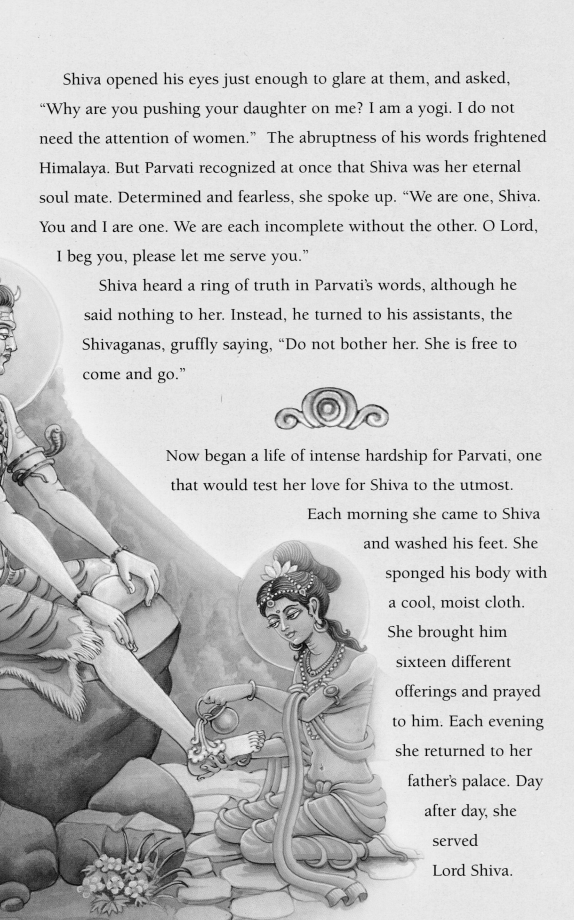

Shiva opened his eyes just enough to glare at them, and asked, "Why are you pushing your daughter on me? I am a yogi. I do not need the attention of women." The abruptness of his words frightened Himalaya. But Parvati recognized at once that Shiva was her eternal soul mate. Determined and fearless, she spoke up. "We are one, Shiva. You and I are one. We are each incomplete without the other. O Lord, I beg you, please let me serve you."

Shiva heard a ring of truth in Parvati's words, although he said nothing to her. Instead, he turned to his assistants, the Shivaganas, gruffly saying, "Do not bother her. She is free to come and go."

Now began a life of intense hardship for Parvati, one that would test her love for Shiva to the utmost.

Each morning she came to Shiva and washed his feet. She sponged his body with a cool, moist cloth. She brought him sixteen different offerings and prayed to him. Each evening she returned to her father's palace. Day after day, she served Lord Shiva.

Shiva remained deep in meditation and
took no notice of her, but Parvati's devotion
melted the hearts of all the other gods.
Indra, the king of the lesser gods, was
especially concerned for her. He
decided to ask his friends Kama and
Rati to help. When Kama and his
wife, Rati, danced, the air overflowed
with love's ardor and nature burst
joyfully into spring. And when Kama
aimed his magical flowery arrow,
whomever he hit became
filled with love's desire.

"Kama," Indra said urgently,
"please do something. Shiva must be
made to notice Parvati. Her love
cannot go in vain."

"Of course," Kama said,
jumping to his feet and grabbing
Rati's hand. "Rati and I would
do anything for Parvati's
happiness."

As Kama tiptoed around Shiva and found a hiding place from which to shoot his arrow, springtime awoke. Birds sang; their hatchlings chirped. Flowers blossomed and their sweet fragrance was carried on gentle, cool breezes. Love was everywhere—even the cruelest and most barren of hearts could not ignore the stirrings of desire.

Shiva, sensing the change in the air, suspected that Kama was somewhere nearby. But before he could investigate, Parvati, dressed in fresh garlands, appeared before him. *Oh dear, Parvati looks more beautiful than ever,* thought Shiva. Then he looked around to see Kama peeking through the bushes, aiming a floral arrow straight at his heart.

Shiva was furious that his focus and concentration had been disrupted. He turned to face Kama and with one glance he destroyed the magic of the arrow. Then the third eye in the middle of Shiva's forehead opened and a bolt of fire shot forth, consuming the unfortunate Kama in a puff of smoke. Rati let out a pitiful cry and ran desperately for help. The gods were horrified to see Kama come to such a fiery end, but there was nothing they could do. Determined to return to his meditation, Shiva vanished from the site.

Heartbroken, Parvati returned to her parents' house. They appealed to Narada for help.

"I have tried so hard!" Parvati told Narada. "What more can I possibly do to win the heart of my beloved Shiva?"

Narada answered in a soothing voice. "You must meditate on his name. Do nothing but chant *Om Namah Shivaya* and do not lose hope. For you, Parvati, nothing is impossible."

Thus began the most severe test for Parvati. To prepare herself, she discarded her jewelry and ornaments, replacing them with simple beads. She gave away her garments of soft, lustrous silk, and donned rough handspun cotton. She went out to where she had last seen Shiva, her heart aching with longing. She was determined to do whatever it took to bring him back.

ॐ नमः शिवाय ॐ नमः शिवाय ॐ नमः शिवाय ॐ नमः शिवाय ॐ नमः शिवाय ॐ नमः शिवाय ॐ नमः शि

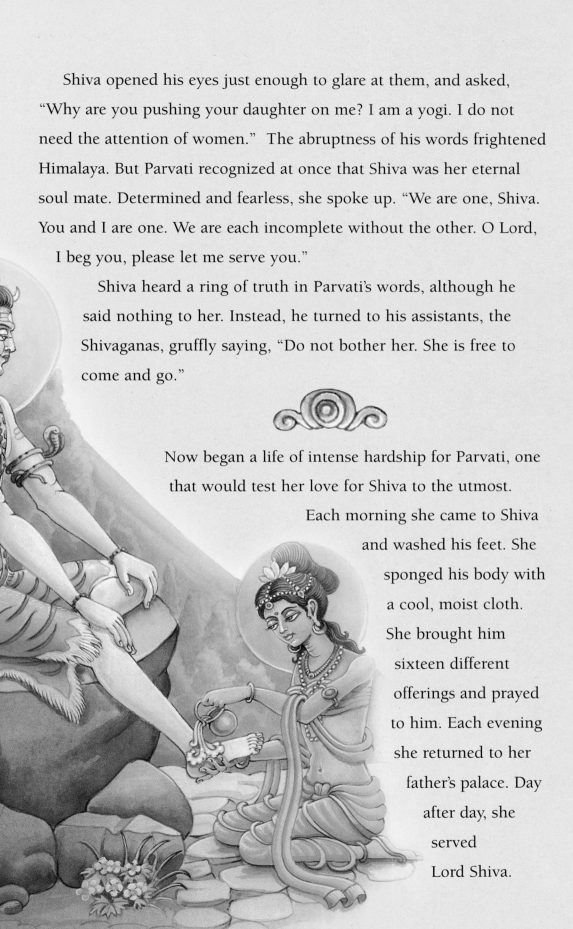

Shiva opened his eyes just enough to glare at them, and asked, "Why are you pushing your daughter on me? I am a yogi. I do not need the attention of women." The abruptness of his words frightened Himalaya. But Parvati recognized at once that Shiva was her eternal soul mate. Determined and fearless, she spoke up. "We are one, Shiva. You and I are one. We are each incomplete without the other. O Lord, I beg you, please let me serve you."

Shiva heard a ring of truth in Parvati's words, although he said nothing to her. Instead, he turned to his assistants, the Shivaganas, gruffly saying, "Do not bother her. She is free to come and go."

Now began a life of intense hardship for Parvati, one that would test her love for Shiva to the utmost.

Each morning she came to Shiva and washed his feet. She sponged his body with a cool, moist cloth. She brought him sixteen different offerings and prayed to him. Each evening she returned to her father's palace. Day after day, she served Lord Shiva.

Parvati embraced all hardships. In the heat of summer she sat in a
ring of blazing fire and chanted "*Om Namah Shivaya.*" In the rainy
season she welcomed the thunderbolts and lightning and continued
chanting through the worst of the storms. In winter she let the snow
bury her body up to her neck, while she kept her mind pure and
focused. "*Om Namah Shivaya, Om Namah Shivaya,*" she chanted, over
and over. But Shiva did not come.

शिवाय ॐ नमः शिवाय ॐ नमः शिवाय ॐ नमः शिवाय ॐ नमः शिवाय ॐ नमः शिवाय ॐ नमः शिवाय ॐ न

Next she spent a year eating nothing but fruits; then for another year she lived on leaves. She gave up food altogether and lived on air and water, then on air alone. Her breath could barely be heard, yet she continued chanting, "*Om Namah Shivaya.*" But Shiva did not come.

Parvati's meditation calmed the beasts around her. The ferocious animals lost their fierceness, while the weaker animals lost their fear. Tigers and lions, rabbits and deer approached quietly and sat together at her feet. The plants and trees produced plenty of fruits and leaves for all the animals and birds, and the forest became an oasis of love and peace. "*Om Namah Shivaya,*" Parvati chanted. But Shiva did not come.

Unable to bear their daughter's pain any longer, Himalaya and Mena came to Parvati. "Daughter, it's no use. Why do you continue? Shiva does not even notice you. Come back to us, dear daughter," they pleaded.

"No," Parvati said. "I will not give up. Shiva will come." She closed her eyes and continued chanting, and her parents turned sadly away. As she focused her mind again, the melodic sound of Parvati's chanting made every cell in her body vibrate with energy. Soon sound energy became heat energy and Parvati began to glow—first like a fierce firefly, then like a brilliant lamp, and finally like a blinding fireball radiating intense waves of heat. Everything around her began to warm up until all the plants and animals and the earth itself felt scorched. And still Parvati chanted to her beloved. Even the gods began to feel that their heavenly home was becoming an inferno. They could take it no longer.

At last Brahma, Vishnu, and all the lesser gods traveled to where Shiva sat. They stood silent and humble, waiting for Shiva to end his meditation. When he finally opened his eyes, Shiva asked, "What brings you here?"

The gods joined their palms together and bowed to Shiva. "Parvati's meditation is burning up the entire universe, dear Lord. She will not give up until you recognize her love for you and marry her."

"I see," said Shiva. "I will consider. . . ."

24

He decided to test Parvati's resolve in person. Dressed as an old Brahmin priest, he appeared before her. "What does your heart desire, my dear young yogin, that you have resorted to such a severe meditation?" he asked.

"My heart belongs to Shiva," Parvati said. "My breath is hanging on only so that I can meet him."

The old man giggled. "That silly Shiva? That ugly, homeless man has nothing to offer a girl like you. He lives in forests and burial grounds. His assistants are horrible ruffians. You'd have a life of certain suffering with him. Change your mind. Even now you have time to save yourself."

Parvati's eyes blazed with fury. "It is a terrible sin to say such things! It is an even greater sin to listen to them!"

Though she knew it was rude to turn away from one's elders, Parvati turned her back on the old Brahmin. She reached to put more wood on the fire so that she could resume her meditation. But the old man grabbed her arm and asked, "Why do you turn away from me, my dearest? You are my eternal beloved. Marry me, please."

Startled, Parvati looked up to see that the old man had vanished. Then her heart leapt, for in his place stood the love of her life, the one for whom she had endured the most difficult of trials. Shiva! At last, Shiva had come!

"Yes," she answered joyfully. "I will marry you."

To complete her happiness, Parvati wanted to tell her parents straight away. They, too, had endured hardship and sadness on her behalf. So she set off for home, anxious to let them know the good news as soon as possible.

Meanwhile, Shiva dressed himself as a street dancer and traveled separately to Himalaya's palace, singing and dancing to his own merry drumbeat. Mena treated the dancer with hospitality, and even brought him precious gifts, but he asked for only one thing—to be married to Parvati. "I am afraid that is not possible," said Mena. "My daughter has waited all her life to marry Shiva. She will not marry a street dancer like you. Please go." The dancer rejected the gifts and continued to dance. "I am here to ask Parvati's hand in marriage," he insisted.

Himalaya at length grew annoyed with the dancer, and asked his soldiers to throw the man out. "Grab him!" he said. But Shiva blazed with the brilliance of a thousand suns, and no one could touch him. "Push him!" Himalaya said. But Shiva whirled in place, as solid and heavy as all the mountains put together, and no one could budge him.

Then all at once Himalaya, Mena, Parvati, and everyone else there fell under a wondrous spell. They saw Lord Vishnu with his conch, discus, mace, and lotus flower. They saw the four-faced, wise Brahma. They saw the three-eyed Shiva with his trident and moon. They saw the entire cosmos in a great swirl of bright energy all around the mysterious dancer and their eyes were opened. Shiva himself, Lord of All Gods, was dancing joyfully in the courtyard, asking Mena and Himalaya for the hand of their daughter, Parvati.

The devoted parents held a glorious wedding for the couple and when the festivities ended, saw them off to the blissful Mount Kailash. As Mena and Himalaya waved farewell, their eyes shone with happiness. Their beloved daughter had finally won the heart of Shiva.

Note to Parents and Teachers

Parvati and Shiva are one of the central couples of Hindu mythology. Each is the perfect complement to the other. As an aspect of the great mother goddess Adishakti, Parvati brings forth and nurtures life. Shiva, on the other hand, is often known as the god of destruction. In that ruthless aspect he must destroy life in order to keep the forces of the universe in balance. Western religious traditions are dualistic, viewing forces as either good or evil. The Hindu tradition takes a more holistic view. Neither creation nor destruction is seen as inherently good or bad—it is the balance between the two that is important.

The story of Parvati's efforts to win Shiva's heart is just one in a vast web of interconnected stories about the Hindu pantheon. Another story in that web provides context for this one. In that story a powerful and destructive demon named Tarakasura has tricked Brahma into giving him a boon—he can be killed only by a son of Shiva. Knowing that the childless Shiva is a wandering ascetic, Tarakasura doesn't see any sons on the horizon. So the boon renders him all but immortal, which means that the forces of destruction are in danger of spinning out of control. When Adishakti comes to Earth as Mena's daughter, Parvati, her greater purpose is to produce a son by Shiva who will be able to kill the demon and restore balance to the universe. But first she must convince Shiva to marry her.

Parvati's courtship story, taken from the *Shiva Purana,* is a story of archetypal perseverance. With the survival of the universe at stake, she knows that there is plenty riding on the success or failure of her mission. Also, as his eternal opposite, she loves Shiva with a steadfast and unshakeable devotion. Hence she has the motivation to confront all obstacles until she reaches her goal.

Parvati's story could spark an interesting discussion with children about identifying and pursuing the things that really matter to them. Parvati is in the fortunate position of possessing a clear and heartfelt goal, but, lacking such clarity, how does one figure out what would make the heart truly happy? What goal could be so important to a child that he or she would do anything to reach it? In order to shut out competing distractions and focus her intent, Parvati uses the Hindu device of reciting a mantra. How might today's child maintain focus toward a goal in the face of the inevitable distractions and discouragements? There are, of course, as many answers to these questions as there are children on Earth.

About the Illustrations

The original illustrations for *How Parvati Won the Heart of Shiva* are wash paintings done in both transparent watercolors and opaque tempera paints. The artist created each piece following a traditional Indian process.

He began with transparent watercolors and painted each picture in several steps. First he outlined the figures; then he filled them in, using three tones for each color to achieve a three-dimensional effect; and finally he applied the background colors. After each step he had to "fix" the painting by pouring water over it until only the paint absorbed by the paper remained.

Then the artist was ready to apply the wash, which is done with opaque tempera paints mixed to a consistency between thin honey and boiled milk. Wetting the painting first, he applied the tempera paint to the surface until the whole painting appeared to be behind a colored fog. While the wash color was still wet, he took a dry brush and removed it from the faces, hands, and feet of the figures.

He let the wash dry completely, then poured water over it to fix the colors again. Many of the paintings received several washes and fixes before the right color tone was achieved. The wash color is important because it sets the emotional tone of the entire painting. Finally, the artist went back in and redefined the delicate line work of the piece, allowing the painting to reemerge from within the clouds of wash.

To give children an opportunity for hands-on participation in this ancient art form, we have included a line drawing of Parvati and Shiva on the following page. Feel free to trace or photocopy the image for children to color.